Dear Parent:

Congratulations! Your child is taking the first steps on an exciting journey. The destination? Independent reading!

P9-CQG-156

STEP INTO READING® will help your child get there. The program offers five steps to reading success. Each step includes fun stories and colorful art. There are also Step into Reading Sticker Books, Step into Reading Math Readers, Step into Reading Phonics Readers, Step into Reading Write-In Readers, and Step into Reading Phonics Boxed Sets—a complete literacy program with something to interest every child.

Learning to Read, Step by Step!

 Ready to Read   Preschool–Kindergarten
• big type and easy words • rhyme and rhythm • picture clues
For children who know the alphabet and are eager to begin reading.

 Reading with Help   Preschool–Grade 1
• basic vocabulary • short sentences • simple stories
For children who recognize familiar words and sound out new words with help.

 Reading on Your Own   Grades 1–3
• engaging characters • easy-to-follow plots • popular topics
For children who are ready to read on their own.

 Reading Paragraphs   Grades 2–3
• challenging vocabulary • short paragraphs • exciting stories
For newly independent readers who read simple sentences with confidence.

 Ready for Chapters   Grades 2–4
• chapters • longer paragraphs • full-color art
For children who want to take the plunge into chapter books but still like colorful pictures.

STEP INTO READING® is designed to give every child a successful reading experience. The grade levels are only guides. Children can progress through the steps at their own speed, developing confidence in their reading, no matter what their grade.

Remember, a lifetime love of reading starts with a single step!

Special thanks to Vicki Jaeger, Monica Okazaki, Kathleen Warner, Emily Kelly,
Sarah Quesenberry, Carla Alford, Julia Phelps, Tanya Mann, Rob Hudnut, Shelley Dvi-Vardhana,
Michelle Cogan, Greg Winters, Taia Morley, and Dynamo Limited

Published in the United States by Random House Children's Books, a division of Random House,
Inc., 1745 Broadway, New York, NY 10019, and in Canada by Random House of Canada Limited,
Toronto.

Step into Reading, Random House, and the Random House colophon are registered trademarks of
Random House, Inc.

Visit us on the Web!
www.StepIntoReading.com
www.randomhouse.com/kids
www.barbie.com

Educators and librarians, for a variety of teaching tools, visit us at
www.randomhouse.com/teachers

Library of Congress Cataloging-in-Publication Data
Man-Kong, Mary.
Barbie : a fashion fairytale / adapted by Mary Man-Kong ; based on the original screenplay
by Elise Allen ; illustrated by Dynamo Limited.
p. cm.
ISBN 978-0-375-86697-5 (trade) — ISBN 978-0-375-96697-2 (lib. bdg.)
I. Allen, Elise. II. Dynamo Limited. III. Barbie, a fashion fairytale (Motion picture). IV. Title.
PZ7.M31215Baj 2010 [E]—dc22 2010011551

Printed in the United States of America
20 19 18 17 16 15 14 13 12

Barbie™
A Fashion Fairytale

Adapted by Mary Man-Kong

Based on the original screenplay by Elise Allen

Illustrated by Dynamo Limited

Random House 🏠 New York

Barbie is
on a plane.
She is going to Paris.
Her pet poodle
is going,
too.
They will help
Barbie's Aunt Millicent.

Millicent is happy
to see Barbie.
But Millicent is sad,
too.
Her fashion house
is closing forever.

Jacqueline is
a mean dressmaker.
She stole Millicent's
fashion ideas.

Alice is
Millicent's helper.
She makes pretty
dresses.
She does not want
Millicent's store
to close.

Barbie and Alice

find a secret wardrobe.

Glimmer, Shimmer,
and Shyne come out.
They are the Flairies!
Their magic makes
Alice's dress sparkle.

Alice and Barbie

love it!

A lady buys
the sparkling dress.
Barbie has an idea.

They will have
a fashion show.
They will
save Millicent's!

Alice and Barbie
work hard.
They make
lovely dresses.

The Flairies make
the dresses
extra pretty!

Jacqueline wants
the Flairies
to make <u>her</u> dresses
sparkle.

She and her helper
kidnap the Flairies!

But the Flairies do not
like Jacqueline's dresses.
The magic will not last.

Jacqueline plans her own
fashion show anyway.

Barbie and Alice are done!

Millicent loves
their dresses.

The Flairies are trapped.
They light up
Jacqueline's store.

The pets save them!

Glimmer, Shimmer,
and Shyne are free!

Jacqueline starts
her fashion show.
But the magic
stops working.

Her fashions turn
into trash!
The show
is a flop.

Millicent starts
her fashion show.
Many people come.

Barbie peeks
at the crowd.
Alice knows Barbie
will be a great model.

Barbie walks
down the runway.
The Flairies make
Barbie's dress
glimmer, shimmer,
and shine.

Millicent's fashion show
is a hit!

Barbie and her friends
thank the Flairies.
Together,
they saved Millicent's
fashion house!